This
Orchard book
belongs to

_____

_____

For Beth, Iain, Norman and Sheila
MM

For Tom and Harrison
AA

ORCHARD BOOKS

First published in Great Britain in 2011
by Orchard Books
First published in paperback in 2012

6 8 10 12 14 15 13 11 9 7

Text © Margaret Mayo 2011
Illustrations © Alex Ayliffe 2011

A CIP catalogue record for this book
is available from the British Library.

ISBN 978 1 40831 251 3

Printed and bound in China

Orchard Books
An imprint of Hachette Children's Group
Part of The Watts Publishing Group Limited
Carmelite House, 50 Victoria Embankment, London EC4Y 0DZ

An Hachette UK Company
www.hachette.co.uk
www.hachettechildrens.co.uk

# Zoom, Rocket, Zoom!

Margaret Mayo & Alex Ayliffe

ORCHARD

# Mighty rockets

are good at zoom, zoom, zooming,

5 4 3 2 1 and . . .

LIFT OFF! Launching!

whoo–oom!

Up they go, zooming.
Blasting into space.

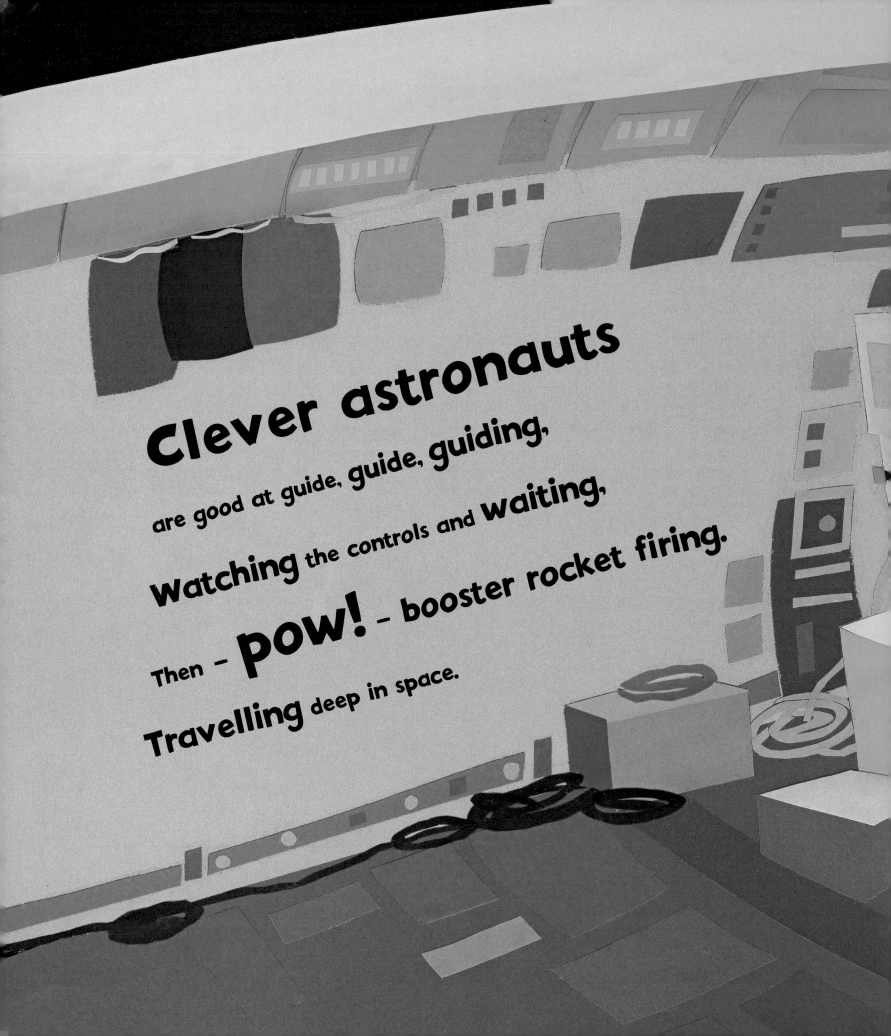

**Clever astronauts**
are good at guide, guide, guiding,
Watching the controls and **waiting,**
Then – **pow!** – booster rocket firing.
Travelling deep in space.

# Lunar modules

are good at **tricky moon landings.**

They leave the spaceship, **swooping, descending,**

Spidery legs ready for – **Bam!** – safe landing.
Touching down in space.

**Excited astronauts** are good at moon walking.

Bouncing, bounding . . . **Oops!** No falling,

As they **SCOOP** up moon rocks, carefully **collecting.**
They can **WORK** in space.

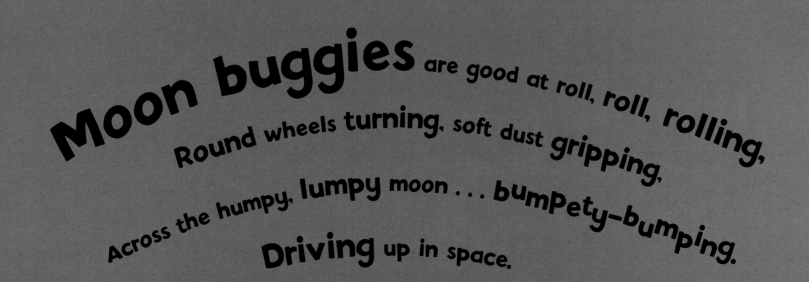

**Moon buggies** are good at roll, roll, rolling,
Round wheels turning, soft dust gripping,
Across the humpy, lumpy moon . . . bumpety-bumping.
**Driving** up in space.

# Space shuttles

are good at **big** loads moving.

They hurtle upwards, **booming**, **thundering**,

Off to a **space station** for fast unloading.

**Carrying** tools through space.

**Space stations**
are good places for living,
Somewhere for eating, working and sleeping,
And – **whoopee!** – weightless **somersaulting.**
A **home** while up in space.

Bold astronauts are good at space walking.
They have **fun** . . .
arms waving . . . slowly moving . . . almost dancing,

And they can work,
building and repairing.
Floating up in space.

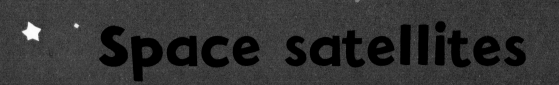

# Space satellites

are good at **round-the-earth orbiting,**

**Taking** pictures for **weather forecasting,**

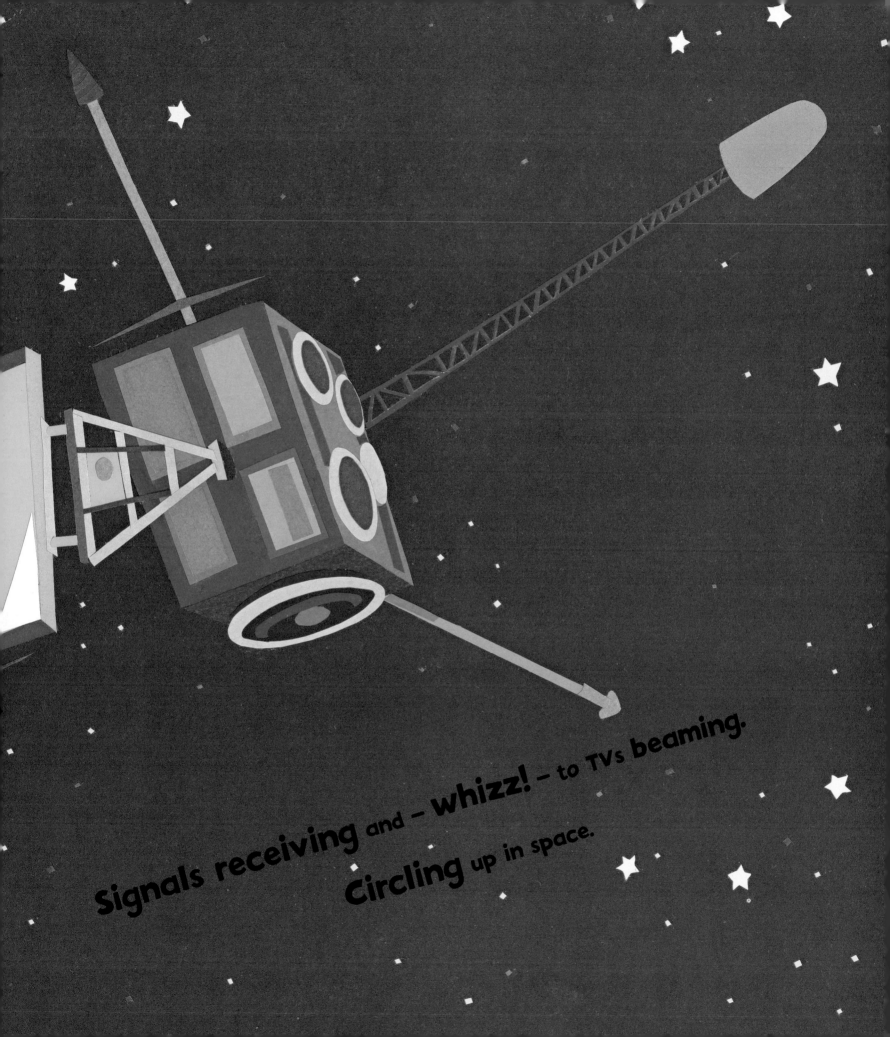

Signals receiving and – whizz! – to TVs beaming.
Circling up in space.

# Robot spacecraft

are good at speed, **speed, speeding,**

**Powered** by the **sun,** they keep on **flying,**

Reaching distant **planets** and even **landing.**

**Moving fast** through space.

# Robot rovers

are **good** at roam, **roam, roaming.**

They **trundle** over Mars, **searching, measuring,**

Red deserts **finding** and mountains **discovering.**

**Exploring** deep in space.

When the **night** has **come** and the **moon** shines bright,

Reflecting down to **earth** our **sun's** great **light** –

Become a **space explorer!** Watch the **stars** in the **sky!**

And look out for **satellites** . . . just slowly gliding by!